BIG RIGS

MEG GREVE

CREATIVE EDUCATION • CREATIVE PAPERBACKS

CONT

ENTS

I SEE A BIG RIG.

This truck drives on highways.

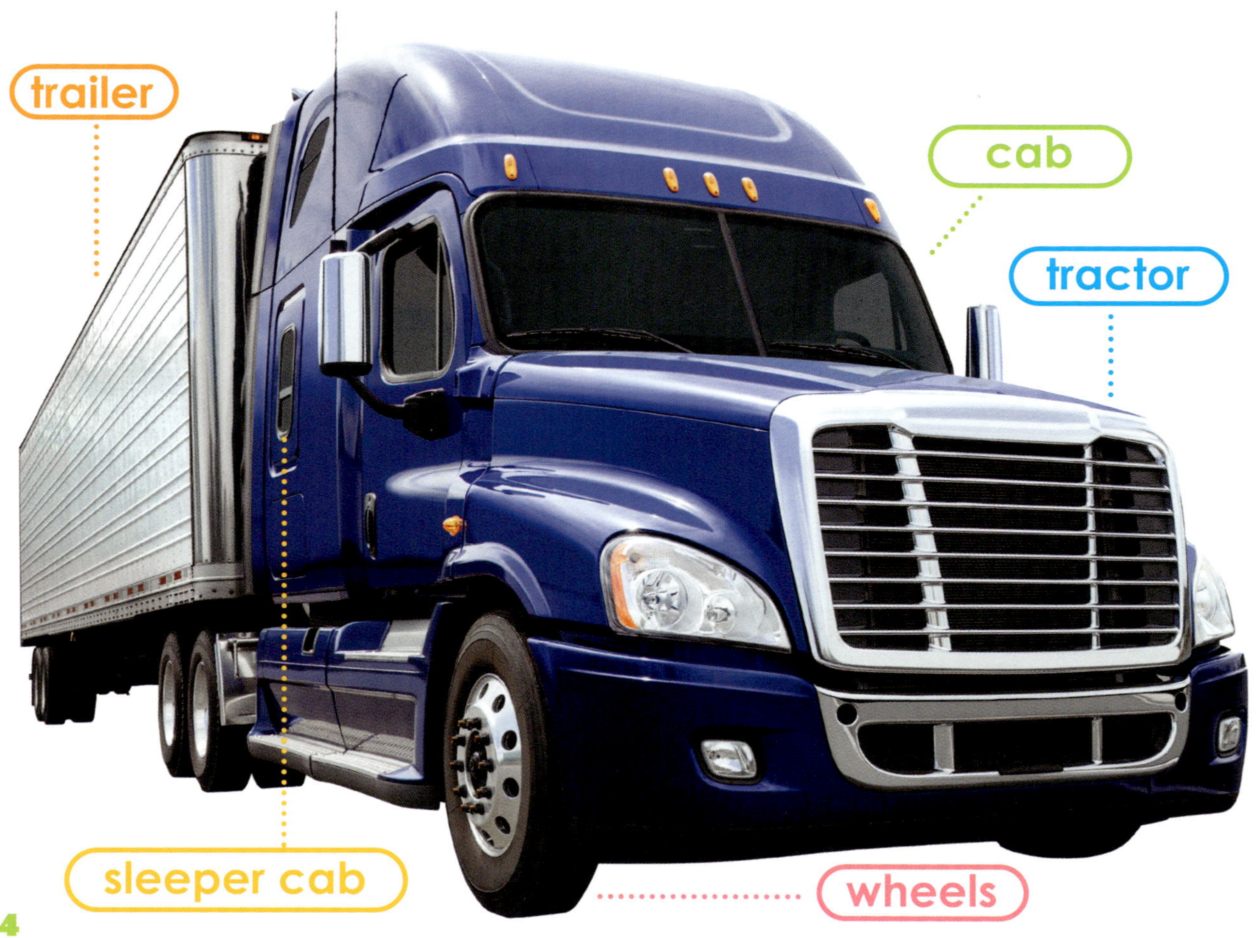

A big rig is also called a semitruck.
Some have 18 wheels!
OVERSIZE LOAD

Big rigs can
carry a lot.

They might <u>haul</u> food, logs, or even animals.

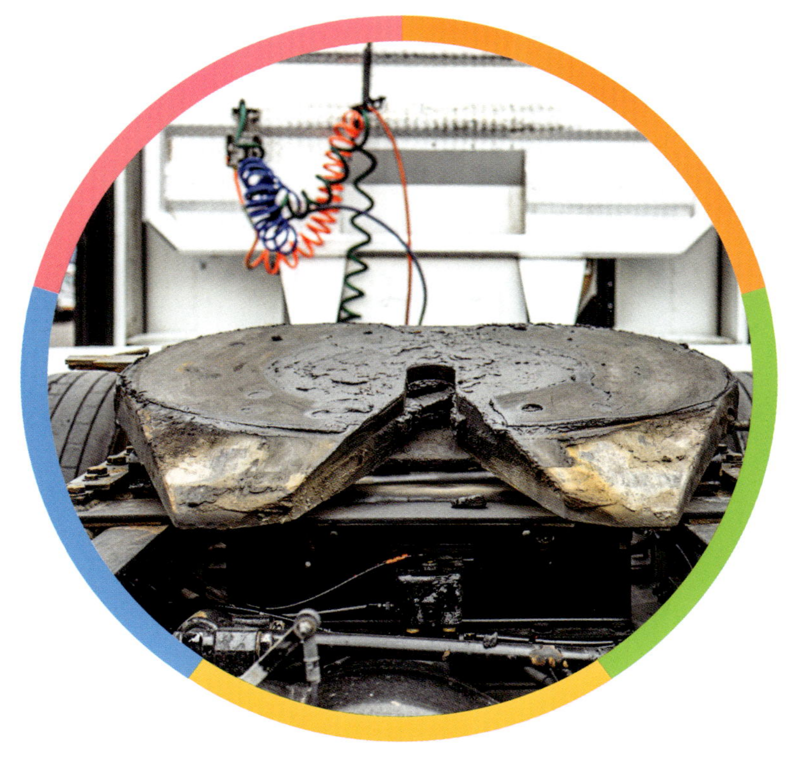

A **plate** **called** **the** fifth wheel connects the tractor and the trailer.

The trailer and tractor fit together like a puzzle.

She drives with
a huge steering
wheel.

The driver yawns. He pulls over. He climbs into the sleeper cab.

After a rest, he will keep trucking!

MAKE A
NOISE
WAH!

Can you make the sounds
of a big rig?

Listen to these sounds:

https://www.youtube.com/
shorts/U4oTyATf7iE

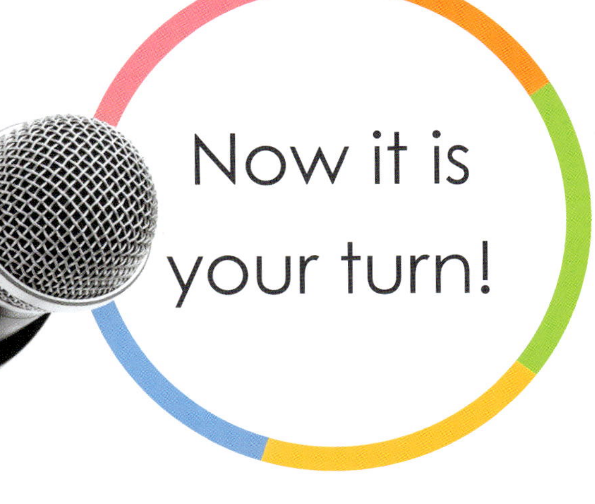

BIG RIG WORDS

haul: to pick up and move

highways: large roads that connect cities and towns

sleeper cab: the area in a truck where the driver can sleep

steering wheel: the wheel that the driver turns to guide or steer the truck

READING CORNER

Gall, Chris. *Big Rig Rescue!*. New York: Norton Young Readers, 2021.

Leed, Percy. *Big Rigs: A First Look*. Minneapolis, Minn.: Lerner Publications, 2023.

Schuh, Mari. *Semitrucks*. Mankato, Minn.: Capstone, 2021.

INDEX

PUBLISHED BY CREATIVE EDUCATION AND CREATIVE PAPERBACKS
P.O. Box 227, Mankato, Minnesota 56002
Creative Education and Creative Paperbacks
are imprints of The Creative Company
www.thecreativecompany.us

LIBRARY OF CONGRESS CATALOGING-IN-PUBLICATION DATA
Names: Greve, Meg, author.
Title: Big rigs / by Meg Greve.
Description: Mankato, Minnesota : Creative Education and Creative Paperbacks, [2025] | Series: Starting out | Includes bibliographical references and index. | Audience: Ages 4-7 | Audience: Grades K-1 | Summary: "Big rigs will introduce budding book learners to a noisy, colorful world with this new Starting Out title. Colorful photos, labeled diagrams, 'Make a Noise' section, glossary, and more ignite a passion for learning"-- Provided by publisher.
Identifiers: LCCN 2023059412 (print) | LCCN 2023059413 (ebook) | ISBN 9798889891666 (library binding) | ISBN 9781682775516 (paperback) | ISBN 9798889891789 (ebook)
Subjects: LCSH: Tractor trailer combinations--Juvenile literature. | Truck trailers--Juvenile literature. | CYAC: Tractor trailer. | LCGFT: Instructional and educational works.
Classification: LCC TL230.15 .G7435 2025 (print) | LCC TL230.15 (ebook) | DDC 629.224--dc23/eng/20240129
LC record available at https://lccn.loc.gov/2023059412
LC ebook record available at https://lccn.loc. gov/2023059413

DESIGN AND PRODUCTION
Design by Rhea Magaro
Production by Beeline Media and Design
Art direction by Tom Morgan
Printed in the United States of America

PHOTOGRAPHS by Getty Images (ryasick, Jetta Productions Inc, Colorblind Images LLC), Shutterstock (Michael Shake, freestore 839, Nerthuz, Michael O'Keene, Bob Pool, Siwakorn1933, Vitpho, Africa Studio, Karl R. Martin, Bohbeh, Masekesam)